JASPER
The Drummin' Boy

Margaret
Taylor
Burroughs

JASPER
The Drummin' Boy
REVISED EDITION

Illustrations
by
Ted Lewin

FOLLETT PUBLISHING COMPANY
Chicago · New York

SBN   695-44537-5   Titan binding
SBN   695-84537-3   Trade binding

Library of Congress Catalog Card Number: 69-15984
First Printing

TO MY DAUGHTER
GAYLE
AND ALL THE OTHERS

JASPER
The Drummin' Boy

"When our children grow up I want them to be somebody," Mrs. Anderson said to Mr. Anderson. "So, I think Donna Jean should take dancing, and Jasper should take piano lessons."

"That's right," said Mr. Anderson. "But I don't know about Jasper playing the piano."

"Some day he will be a great concert pianist," Mrs. Anderson said with a dreamy look in her eyes. "Why he might even play at Orchestra Hall downtown. That's what I wanted to be when I was young, a concert pianist, but I didn't have the chance. But it will be different with Jasper."

And so, from that day on, every Monday after school Jasper had to go over to Mr. Patton's school of music for his piano lesson.

Mr. Patton wore thick glasses and was always tapping out time. Jasper thought that he must tap time in his sleep.

"Now look here, Jasper Anderson," Mr. Patton would say. "You don't at all have your mind on what you are doing. Keep your eyes on the music and keys and not on that drum over in the corner. Now let's try this all over again. One . . . two . . . three . . . one . . . two . . . three. . . ." Jasper stared obediently at the piano keys.

He tried hard. He plunked and plinked and plunked and plinked. Down went the white keys, and up went the black keys. Down went the black keys, and up went the white keys over and over again. "Jasper Anderson," Mr. Patton said as he took off his glasses. "Why on earth do you pound so hard? You make this piano sound like a drum."

"I'm sorry, Mr. Patton," Jasper said.

That evening Mrs. Anderson said to her husband, "Mr. Patton called to say that Jasper isn't paying enough attention to his music lessons, and he keeps pounding the piano as if it were a drum. I wish you would speak to him."

"I'll speak to him again, Alice," Mr. Anderson said in a hopeless voice as he looked up at the orchestra picture which hung over the piano. "You know Jasper didn't steal that desire to play the drum. He got it from his grandpa, my daddy who played with the great Duke Oliver Band. He was some drummer! Jasper took that talent from him. Maybe you should have let the boy take drumming instead of piano."

"Jasper is going to be a concert pianist, nothing else but," said Mrs. Anderson, who had played the piano in her father's church when she was young. "If it hadn't been for you giving him that drum for Christmas that time he might be able to keep his mind on the piano now. It's all your fault."

12

"But Alice," Mr. Anderson said. "Didn't I lock the drum away? And what did he do? He found an old nail keg and made a drum out of that. Don't I take away every pair of sticks he gets? How was I to know that he would be marked for life? I thought a drum would be just the thing for a boy."

"That's true. But it's no need for a boy to go clean drum-crazy. Well, I'm sure he didn't get it from my side of the family."

"I guess the Andersons will have to take the blame. He really didn't steal it, you know."

"James Anderson, are you taking that boy's side? The first thing you know, the neighbors will be complaining about his noise, and you know how hard it is to find a place to live when you have children. Now you do something about Jasper."

"I'll see about him, Alice," Mr. Anderson said as he folded his newspaper to the sports page.

On Sunday, on the way to service at Mount Olive Church, Jasper made up his mind to be good so that he could go to hear Stomp King, the famous drummer who was playing at the Regal that week. It was easier to be good if you were alone, so when Momma and Papa and Donna Jean turned in to their regular pew, Jasper marched on past, up to an empty pew right near the front, and sat down by himself.

Jasper sat as quiet as a mouse while Reverend Elder preached the sermon. The sun streaming in through the colored glass windows was like a rainbow, blue and green and red and yellow. It looked to Jasper as if Reverend Elder was standing in a garden with all those flowers and ferns around the pulpit. Reverend Elder was brown and plump and his gray hair almost came down over his ears. Above the choir loft was a large picture of Jesus in the garden. Why did Jesus look so sad? Why did he have such long hair? And why did he wear those

14

long robes? Jasper wondered.

At last the sermon was over. The gospel choir in their black robes and white collars had stood up to sing. It was hard to keep still when the Mount Olive gospel choir sang.

Before Jasper knew it, he was drumming with his feet on the pew ahead, right along with the choir. "Joshua fit the battle of Jericho, Jericho, Jericho." Jasper kept right up with them. He could see the walls tumbling, tumbling down. Joshua was quite a fighter!

The deep bass singers began to fidget in the back row. The heavy alto singers looked from side to side. The high tenor singers looked at the bass singers as if it were their fault. The bass singers frowned at the sopranos. The sopranos glared at the altos, and the choir director scowled at all of them.

He had stopped his directing to listen. Now motioning to the singers to hum, he turned and looked across the pulpit at Jas-

16

per, who was still drumming away.

Reverend Elder looked at Jasper, with his eyebrows raised. Mrs. Anderson, in the eighth row back, frowned and nudged Mr. Anderson. Donna Jean was giggling.

The first thing Jasper knew Papa had come up and taken a firm hold of his shoulder and was sitting down beside him with a look which meant there would be no show-fare to hear Stomp King at the Regal. Then Jasper saw that a lot of people were craning their necks and half-standing to see what was happening. Jasper scrunched away down in his seat, as far out of sight as he could get. Now he knew it would be a long time before Papa would let him have his drum back.

When service was over, as the people filed out, Reverend Elder made his way down to Mr. and Mrs. Anderson. He looked at Jasper. "Ahem," he cleared his throat. "Mr. and Mrs. Anderson," he said. "You will just have to do something about Jasper.

You heard how he got the choir all mixed up in their timing. Either he will have to stop that drumming or you'll have to leave him at home."

"Yes, Reverend Elder," Mrs. Anderson apologized. "I can promise you it won't happen again."

"Listen, young man," his father said, "I'll take care of you for embarrassing your mother and me and Donna Jean like that. You wait until we get home."

"Aw, Papa," Jasper said. "I'm sorry. I was only helping Joshua to tumble the walls down."

When they got home, Mr. Anderson had a very serious talk with Jasper about what had happened in church. Jasper was truly sorry. He didn't like to remember it.

"I guess I forgot where I was, Papa," he said humbly. "And I did want to help Joshua win that battle."

"So that you won't forget next time,"

Mr. Anderson said, "I think it will be best for you to stay at home this afternoon. You won't need showfare. And no TV either."

"I won't need it, Papa," Jasper said, and all visions of seeing the Stomp King show faded.

"But after dinner," Mr. Anderson said, "you may play quietly in the back yard for a while."

"Thank you, Papa," Jasper said.

Jasper was in the back yard. He was thinking deep to himself. This old world makes me mad, he thought. Every time . . . every time I get a pair of sticks they disappear. Somebody takes them. Maybe it's Donna Jean. I bet it's Papa who takes them. And Papa hid my drum away and I can't find it. "Well," he said aloud, "I'm going to make myself one more pair of sticks and nobody will take these. And I will play them on the washtub drum I'm going to make."

Jasper poked around the yard for a few

minutes with his hands deep in his pockets. There should be some stray wood around. He walked over to the gate. Good! There was a small board. He picked it up and weighed it in his hands. "This will do if I split it," he said. He looked around. The basement door was open. Mr. Jellife wouldn't mind if he went in there and split that little board with his hatchet. Mr. Jellife wasn't there. Jasper came out balancing the two pieces of wood, one in each hand. He felt in his pocket for his scout knife.

Jasper climbed up on the fence close to the shade tree and started to whittle first on one and then on the other. Zip . . . zipp, zipp. . . . The shavings began to fly fast in all directions. It wasn't long before the sticks began to take shape. He balanced them again. They were just right for flipping up in the air too. Then he began to smooth them off. If only he had a piece of sandpaper. . . .

Jasper began to think about his best

friends, Butch and Ike. He and Butch and Ike were the only members of the Three X's club. They were the only ones in all of Chicago, in the whole world who knew the supreme secret handshake. Butch was fat and jolly and never got angry. Ike was tall and thin. He had high cheekbones and a tuft of hair over his forehead that stood straight up. It made him look like the African warrior who sat in Jasper's geography book beating a drum. Jasper liked that picture. Jasper wished that Momma would let him grow his hair like that, but Momma had said, "No, Jasper Anderson, you are not an African warrior. You are an African-American. I just don't think that kind of hairdo would look good on a concert pianist. Maybe when you get older."

Jasper wondered what Butch and Ike were doing now. I bet they've gone to the show at the Regal, he said to himself. I wish I was with them. I would love to be seeing Stomp King leading the orchestra and playing the drums right this minute . . . These sticks need a little more curve . . . I hope Butch and Ike haven't forgotten about Saturday. Gee I wish . . . I wish that I lived back in history. I wish I was an African drummer. I would be the master drummer. I would play the talking drums and send messages all over Africa. I could be like Barzillai Lew, the black drummer boy in the Revolutionary War. I would be a minuteman like Peter Salem. I would be like Grandpa Anderson playing drums in Duke Oliver's Windy City Band.

Jasper balanced the sticks again. These were going to be good. He flipped them in the air a couple of times and caught them the way he had seen Stomp King do on TV. Stomp King was some drummer. He was almost as good as Grandpa Anderson, Jasper thought. He could beat a drum with his eyes shut. He could do all sorts of flips and stunts, and he never missed a beat.

Someday . . . someday Jasper thought,

23

I will be a great drummer like Stomp King and then Momma will be proud of me. She will be sorry that she made me practice the piano instead of the drum. She'll be sorry! Papa would let him have the medal that Grandpa won when he played in The Battle of the Bands, long before Jasper was born. He would wear it in the Bud Billiken parade down Dr. Martin Luther King Drive. The neighborhood boys would boast about how they had lived in the same block with Jasper Anderson, the great drummer.

Jasper looked proudly at the sticks he had made. "These are fine drumsticks," he said. "I think I will warm them up to take the newness off for Saturday." He began first a slow rhythm, da da da, da da da, and then he picked up speed, faster, faster. He sounded just like a train right there on the back yard fence. This was a streamline train and he was the engineer.

"Hey there, Jasper," Mr. Jellife called as he came around the side of the building.

"Get down off that fence with all that noise. And pick up all that trash you put there, too."

"All right, Mr. Jellife," Jasper said as he climbed down from the fence. "Well, this train can't go no further." He began to pick up the shavings.

"What's that you said?" asked Mr. Jellife. "You know your folks don't allow no sassy talk."

"I'm sorry, I wasn't sassing, Mr. Jellife, I said my train has to stop right here."

"Boy, who's talking about a train?" Mr. Jellife shook his head. "That boy Jasper is a pain."

With his sticks in hand, Jasper walked slowly up the stairs to their second-floor back porch. He sat down in the swing and began going to and fro. He looked at his sticks. I wonder what kind of sound these would make on the porch rail, he thought. He began. This time he was playing the drums at the Regal with Stomp King. There he was seated in the center of the stage behind a bright shiny drum set, complete with the bass, snare, and cymbals. The garbage can made a fine bass drum. The lid, strung from the clothesline, made a fine cymbal. Jasper began to play.

"Hey you, Jasper," Mrs. Clendenning, the third-floor neighbor called down. "Stop that drumming and banging. You know your folks don't stand for all that racket! Do you want to wear all the paint off the porch rail? Besides, my husband works at night and has to get his sleep. Now, you stop that noise right now."

"All right, Mrs. Clendenning," Jasper said, "I didn't realize I was playing so loud. I was playing drums at the Regal Theatre."

"Who said anything about The Regal Theatre? That boy Jasper is a card," Mrs. Clendenning said as she went back into her kitchen.

Through the screen door, Jasper could see Momma come into the kitchen. He quickly shoved the drumsticks inside his shirt.

"Jasper! Jasper! Come this very minute and practice your piano lesson. Oh, I could weep every time I think about how you acted in church this morning."

"I'm coming, Momma," Jasper said, and he kicked at the garbage can and placed the lid back on it.

He walked slowly through the house to the parlor. He caught a glimpse of Donna Jean in the family room looking at TV. She never seemed to do anything wrong. What a kid sister! He plopped himself down on the piano stool and started to go through his finger exercises. Plink plank plunk! Plink plank plunk! Plinketty, planketty, plunk, plunk! His fingers thumped heavily along the keys. I wish this was a drum, I wish it was a Congo drum or a set of bongos or jazz drums.

He looked up at the picture that hung on the striped wall over the piano. It was

the colored photograph of Grandpa Anderson and the popular Duke Oliver Windy
City Band. Grandpa was in the center behind the big drum. If you looked real close
you could see the medal that he won in The
Battle of the Bands.

"You want to try to be like him," Papa
had once said. Then Papa had told him
about the medal which was down in the bottom of the old family trunk. "That medal
will belong to you whenever you do a worthy
deed, Jasper," Papa had said.

Jasper had tried very hard to do a
worthy deed but he always seemed to have
bad luck. He knew the main reason was his
drumming. But he just couldn't help himself. After all, Grandpa was a good drummer, and it couldn't be wrong to want to be
like Grandpa. Momma didn't seem to
understand, but Papa sometimes did.

Jasper looked at the picture for a long
time. Suddenly, it seemed that Grandpa was
smiling at him. Duke Oliver and the other

musicians were smiling, too. Then Grandpa crooked his finger and beckoned to Jasper. The next thing Jasper knew he was walking right into the picture, through the glass and frame and all.

All of the band members stood holding their instruments and smiling. It seemed as if they had been waiting for him. Jasper knew the names of some of the instruments. The long skinny black one was the clarinet. The shiny fat one that bulged at the end was the saxophone. The little one that went around in a coil and flared out at the end was the cornet. There were shiny tinkling cymbals and long wailing trombones and high piping piccolos. There were great grandfather tuba horns that coiled around and had big bell mouths. There was a piano and a string bass, too. But most exciting of all, there were the drums. The big bass was in the middle, and there were two smaller snare drums on each side. Behind the big bass drum was Grandpa.

"Why, hello, Jasper," the man with the cornet said. "We have been expecting a visit from you for a long time."

"Now that you have finally come, welcome," Duke Oliver said, bowing low with a wave of his baton. The other musicians crowded around him.

"I am very happy to be here," Jasper said. "Where I live folks just don't seem to appreciate a boy like me." And he told them about the fuss folks were always making and the punishment they gave him just because he wanted to get in a little drum practice.

The musicians shook their heads in sympathy. Duke Oliver said, "No, sir, people these days don't have any appreciation for a boy that's born to be a real drummer."

"This boy is just a chip off the old block," Grandpa said as he came forward proudly. He hoisted Jasper up in his arms and gave him a big hug. Jasper squirmed away.

"What's the matter, son?"

"Your medal, Grandpa, it hurts!"

"We were all proud of winning that medal," Grandpa said. "How did you know about it?"

"Papa told me how you and Mr. Oliver won The Battle of the Bands. He said that you all were great."

"I'll put it away." He took the medal off and slipped it into his coat pocket. Jasper followed it with his eyes.

"I told Butch and Ike and all the boys in the neighborhood how you won that medal," said Jasper.

"It's really nothing much," Grandpa said modestly. "Duke Oliver here gets the credit."

"A good band is just like a ball team," Duke Oliver said. "Everybody has to work together. That's how we won."

"Gee, I'm proud of you all," Jasper said.

"Well, let's have some music," Duke Oliver said. "Son, if your grandpa doesn't mind, you can try out his drums. Let's see if you really are a chip off the old block."

"It is a pleasure," Grandpa said, as he handed his sticks to Jasper and began to adjust the drums. "Let's see how much of an Anderson you are."

"You are the best grandpa in all the world," Jasper said.

"Everyone ready?" The bandmaster held up his baton. "Two . . . three. . . ." The band swung into action.

Jasper could hear the moan of the clarinet, the whistle of the piccolo, the cry of the cornet, and the growl of the tuba. He could hear the lonesome wail of the long trombones and ever so often the tinkling of the cymbals. And throughout the whole piece, he, Jasper Anderson, was rumbling the drums. The other musicians stopped playing and allowed Jasper to do a solo. Grandpa smiled encouragingly at him. Jasper was happy that Grandpa was pleased with his playing. Boom boom boom, rub a dub dub, boom boom boom, rub a dub dub. These drums were wonderful. Just as he was starting to end the piece with a great cannonlike rumble, he felt someone shaking him by the shoulder.

Jasper opened his eyes to see his mother standing over him.

"Jasper," she said, "I sent you up here to practice your lesson and here you are, fast asleep, making a lot of noise rumbling these keys. Your father will hear about this."

"Aw, Momma," Jasper said as he rubbed his eyes and glanced toward the picture, "I didn't have a chance to tell them thanks or good-bye."

"Boy, what on earth are you talking about? Here's some money. Run to the store and get me a head of lettuce. Hurry back. Don't stop on the way, you hear?"

"Yes, Momma."

Jasper walked slowly out of Room 303 and down the corridor to the steps that led

to the outside door. Mrs. Ellis had made
him stay after school again, and this time
she had written a long note for him to take
home to his mother. He was so sad that he
didn't even feel like sliding down the ban-
ister. There wasn't a soul around either,
and he could have taken two or three slides.
He went out into the school yard, where
Butch and Ike were waiting for him. They
were true pals. They never let a fellow down.

"What did she do to you?" Butch asked.

"Oh, she gave me a note to take home,
that's all," Jasper muttered.

"Did she stick it?" Ike asked.

"Yes, she stuck it. But I can just about
guess what she wrote in it."

"Will you get a whipping?" both boys
asked.

"I guess I will."

When they reached Indiana Avenue,
Jasper had to turn off.

"Say, don't forget about Saturday. Are
we still going to be in the street fair up on

47th and King Drive?"

"Sure, we are," said Butch. "The president of the merchants' association said he'd be glad to have us in it."

"You fellows got your instruments ready?" Jasper asked.

"Sure. What about you?"

"I'll have mine ready."

The Three X's shook the secret handshake and went their ways.

When he reached the big red-stone building in the middle of the forty-six-hundred block, Jasper turned in and climbed to the second-floor apartment. As he edged in the door, his mother marched up to meet him.

"Donna Jean brought me the news about your acting up in school today, Jasper Anderson. What is it this time?"

"The teacher sent a note," Jasper said as he handed it to her.

Mrs. Anderson tore open the envelope and read the note. It said: "Dear Mrs.

Anderson. Your son is a very smart child in his studies but there is one thing that he does that I just cannot put up with any longer. He finishes his work, and while the others are working he starts drumming all over everything. When he drums with sticks I take them away from him. The next thing I know he is drumming with his pencil. When I take that away, he uses his fingers. He even uses his feet. And when he isn't doing that, he and his pals, Butch and Ike, are singing do-wop songs in the cloakroom. The principal reports that the three of them have been caught singing and playing bongos in the boys' room, too. Will you and Mr. Anderson please try to do something with Jasper. I give up."

Mrs. Anderson folded the note slowly and said sternly: "Jasper, this is too much, drumming in school! Singing when you should be studying. Your father will certainly take care of you when he gets home. You'd better stay in the house the rest of the afternoon. And absolutely no TV for the rest of the week!"

An hour later Jasper heard Butch and Ike whistling for him downstairs. He waved sadly to them from the window and went off to the parlor and sat down on the piano stool. He looked up at Grandpa Anderson sitting up there behind his drums and that made him feel better.

The thing that Jasper liked best about Butch and Ike was that they never minded hearing him tell about what a fine drummer Grandpa had been and how he had won his medal.

"Gee, Jasper," Butch would say. "Your Grandpa really must have been a great drummer, getting a medal like that."

"He sure must have been a great musician," Ike would say.

"I bet he was better than Stomp King, even," Butch would add.

"Grandpa was truly great," Jasper would admit.

The week passed slowly for Jasper. But he endured it. After all, Saturday was only a day or so away now. A very important meeting of the Three X's was called for Friday after school in Ike's basement. All X's were pledged to be there on their word of honor. "Remember," Ike had said, "come equipped."

It was Saturday noon, and Mrs. Anderson had two bulging grocery bags in her hands. Donna Jean was struggling with a package almost bigger than she.

"Have you seen Jasper, Mr. Jellife?" Mrs. Anderson called.

"I saw him a while back working on something in the basement."

"If you see him, please tell him that I want him right away."

"If I see him, I'll send him straight to you."

Mrs. Anderson unlocked the kitchen door and plumped the heavy bags down on the table. "Now for that cake," she said.

She slipped into her house apron, put the groceries away, and set out the ingredients for her cake. It was to be a three-layer chocolate one, in celebration of the Andersons' fifteenth wedding anniversary. Mr. Anderson was very fond of chocolate cake. It would be a lovely little party with a few close friends. While she was sifting the flour, there came a knock at the door.

"See who it is, Donna Jean. My hands are full of flour."

"Yes, Mommie. It's Mrs. Jenkins, Mommie."

The first-floor neighbor bustled in. "How do, Mrs. Anderson. I just ran up to see if Jasper has finished with my washtub. I need it right now."

"Your washtub! Did Jasper borrow your washtub?"

"Jasper did just that."

"Well, I never! That boy! That boy! Whatever will I do with him? Mrs. Jenkins, if you will just be a little patient, I'll see that he brings your tub right back."

"That will be fine," Mrs. Jenkins said. She threw up her hands as she went out the door. "This younger generation!" she said. "They are something else!"

"If that Jasper isn't the beatin'est boy I ever saw!" his mother said as she broke the eggs into a bowl. "What on earth would he want with Mrs. Jenkins' washtub?" And Mrs. Anderson started churning the egg-beater.

Brr-ring! Brr-ring! Brr-ring!

"Now it's the telephone," she said, wiping her hands and going into the hall to answer it.

"Hello?"

It was Mrs. Spotser, the third floor neighbor.

"What? You need your scrub pail? You say that Jasper borrowed it? Oh, Mrs. Spotser, I didn't know that he did . . . No . . . Well, I'll see that he brings it right back . . .

I'm really very sorry . . . Yes, I will . . . Goodbye." She clicked the receiver back into place.

"Mommie, what's Jasper into now?"

"Don't even mention that boy's name to me! Just imagine! Borrowing things from the neighbors and not returning them. Wait until he gets home!"

She lit the oven. The batter was about ready now. Where were those cake tins? She looked on all pantry shelves. They were not there. She looked in the bottom drawer of the cabinet. They were not there. Where could they be? In the bottom of the stove? No, not there. She was getting a little bit warm. She wiped her hands across her forehead.

"What are you looking for, Mommie?"

"My new cake tins. The new ones I had Jasper to buy for me at the hardware store last week. Where in the world . . . ?"

"If you let me lick the cake bowl, I'll tell you where they are."

44

"Listen, child, if you know where those pans are, you tell me this minute. Tell me!"

"Jasper will call me a tattletale if I do."

"Donna Jean, where are those cake tins?"

"Jasper borrowed all of them. He took them this morning."

"Borrowed my cake tins? What for?"

"He said he had to make something. It's something he and Butch and Ike are doing today. They were talking on the phone."

"This is the end," Mrs. Anderson said, and she was very angry. "Mrs. Jenkins' washtub! Mrs. Spotser's scrub pail! And now my new tins! I'll see that he returns those things right now!"

Her brown eyes flashed as she put a plate over the cake batter and took off her apron. She went out the front door, with Donna Jean following.

"Whatcha gonna do to Jasper, Mommie?" Donna Jean asked.

"I'm going to see that he returns every single thing he borrowed," her mother answered, and her lips were in a very straight line.

She went upstairs and rapped at Mrs. Spotser's door.

"Follow me if you want your scrub pail."

She went downstairs and rapped at Mrs. Jenkins' door.

"Come along if you want your washtub."

The other neighbors, Mrs. Clendenning, Mrs. Amos, and Mrs. Tolliver, opened their doors to see what the commotion was.

"Come along if you have time," Mrs. Anderson called. "This is going to be a sight to see!"

"We'll be coming," they answered.

Mr. Jellife was downstairs mopping the vestibule. "If you're looking for Jasper, I saw him up on Forty-Seventh and King Drive playing music in the merchants' association street fair. He and his pals have built some strange contraptions. They're really drawing a crowd, too. Incidentally, he borrowed my best broom handle."

"Merchants' association street fair, indeed! Just follow me, Mr. Jellife, for your broom handle." Mrs. Anderson's lips were in a very, very straight line now. "After all the money I have spent giving him piano lessons so he could be somebody, here he is drumming on a street corner!"

Down the street they went. Mrs. Anderson walked in front. Then came Mrs. Spotser and Mrs. Jenkins. Next came Mrs. Amos, Mrs. Tolliver, and Mrs. Clendenning. Mr. Jellife and Donna Jean brought up the rear.

When some of the neighborhood boys saw Mrs. Anderson and the neighbors on the way to the street fair, they joined the parade too. On the corner Mrs. Ellis, Jasper's teacher, stood talking to Reverend Elder from Mount Olive. They noticed the little army led by Mrs. Anderson and decided to follow curiously after them.

They approached a crowd of people who were standing on the corner, patting with their feet and snapping their fingers. Merchants all down the block had set up colorful booths before their stores. Surplus wares were being sold to benefit the community civic fund. It was a gala afternoon, and many people were walking up and down and milling around.

"Oh, play it!" one man said.

"How's that for a homemade guitar? It's the funniest thing I ever saw," a woman laughed.

"Children of today really have imagination," an old man said.

"Look at that drum contraption," a big boy said.

The street voices blended in with the sounds coming from the center of the circle. "These boys are good. . . . The fat one blows that jug as if he was playing a million-dollar horn. . . . The skinny one plucks his three-string homemade box as if it was Leadbelly's twelve-string guitar . . . and hasn't the one with the drum got Stomp King down to a T? . . . He sure has. . . . Stomp King should hear him."

Mrs. Anderson and her army drew closer. Ike's guitar whined a steady twang twang twang. Voop . . . voop . . . voop went Butch as he puffed his cheeks in and out.

Jasper's big brown eyes sparkled, and his face was crinkled by a wide smile. His hands clenched the sticks lightly but firmly. His arms looked like windmills as he put his whole heart into the drumming. Boom boom boom boom, roared Mrs. Jenkins' washtub. Thump te thump te thump, echoed Mrs. Spotser's scrub pail. Zing zing zang zing zing zang zing, sang Mrs. Anderson's cake tins as they dangled merrily from Mr. Jel-

life's broom handle.

Every so often Jasper would toss the sticks high in the air, clap his hands and then catch the sticks in perfect time, like Stomp King. Jasper was drumming as he never had before. If Grandpa could only see him now, he would be proud.

Mrs. Anderson and her army pushed themselves right into the center of the crowd.

"There's my washtub!" Mrs. Jenkins said as she noticed the dents in it.

"There's my scrub pail!" Mrs. Spotser said. "It's ruined!"

"My broom handle won't be any good with all those nails in it," Mr. Jellife said.

"My new cake tins!" Mrs. Anderson said as she marched right up to Jasper. "Jasper Anderson! You stop your racket this very minute! Borrowing other people's property! Drumming on the street! After all the money your father and me have spent giving you piano lessons! You are a disgrace to the whole Anderson family."

"That's his mother," someone said. "She's really furious about something."

"Whatcha gonna do to Jasper, Mommie?" Donna Jean asked.

Jasper felt like sinking through the sidewalk.

"Gee, Mrs. Anderson," Butch said. "It wasn't his fault."

"It was our fault," Ike said. "It was my idea. I heard about the street fair and volunteered the services of the Three X's to play."

"We wanted to do something to help raise money for the Community Civic Fund," said Butch, "It's used to fix up the playgrounds, and we kids benefit from it. We just wanted to help, Mrs. Anderson."

The crowd began to giggle. Mrs. Ellis and Reverend Elder didn't even look sorry. Jasper's big brown button eyes slowly filled with tears. He tried not to cry in front of all those people.

Suddenly there was a flurry in the

crowd. The people stopped looking at Jasper and looked at someone else. Jasper felt relieved. He brushed his tears on his sleeve. Even Momma had turned away.

The people began talking all at once.

"It's Stomp King! The famous bandleader! That's the president of the merchants' association with him."

"They were listening all of the time."

"Stomp King is the greatest drummer in the business today."

Stomp King pushed forward into the circle. He was dressed in the latest fashion. Butch and Ike stared at him with their mouths wide open. Jasper stood rooted to the pavement with his head down in shame. He had wanted to see Stomp King, but he hadn't wanted the great drummer to see him like this—in such a state of disgrace.

"We heard about the wonderful job you boys are doing," the president of the merchant's association complimented them. "Your music is attracting a lot of people to

our fair. Stomp King heard about your combo and insisted on coming down to hear you kids in person." Mrs. Anderson was just about to lunge toward Jasper.

"Good afternoon, ma'am. Are these your boys?" Stomp King asked her.

"Yes, this one is, and he is no prize."

"On the contrary, ma'am, you have there a boy of rare talent," Stomp King said. "Of very rare talent. As a matter of fact, I think he has the makings of a great drummer."

Jasper's heart began to thump louder than he had made the washtub thump. He stole a glance up at Stomp King. He looked at his mother. The thin angry line of her lips was disappearing.

"Do you really think he has talent, Mr. er-King?"

"I certainly do, ma'am," Stomp King said. "Has he ever taken any lessons?"

"Oh, he takes lessons, but not exactly on the drum."

56

"By all means, he should have lessons on the drum, too," Stomp King said. "Young people who are engaged in creative activity don't have time to get into trouble. It's wonderful that you and the other parents have encouraged these boys and that the merchants here gave them a chance to be heard. And another thing, Mrs. er-er-"

"Anderson," Jasper's mother said. "Mrs. James Anderson."

"One other thing, Mrs. Anderson. If it will be all right with you and the other boys' parents, I should like for them to be my special guests on the Regal stage at the afternoon show tomorrow. In fact I'd like them to bring these unique instruments and play for the audience." Stomp King pulled some tickets out of his pocket. "Do you think it can be arranged, ma'am?"

Mrs. Anderson thought for a minute. "Well—yes, I think it can be arranged, Mr. King . . . I'm sure it can. I'll get in touch with the other boys' parents, too."

"That's wonderful. Now, here are tickets for the boys and for yourself and a few friends. Yes, this talented lad is going to make you very proud some day. If they keep on playing like this, who knows they might cut a record soon." As he turned to leave, he shook hands with the boys. "I will be expecting you tomorrow, fellows. And you, Jasper, I'm going to let you try out my special drums."

"Oh, Mr. King! Thanks!" Jasper squealed.

"Gee, sir! Gee!" Butch and Ike said.

The crowd began to drift to other parts of the fair down the block. Mrs. Anderson's little army reassembled. The procession started back home. The neighborhood boys ran on ahead. First came Jasper carrying his drum contraption and he was smiling. Next came Mrs. Anderson and she was smiling too. Then came Butch with his jug and Ike with his guitar. Butch and Ike were smiling big wide smiles. They were followed by Mrs.

Jenkins and Mrs. Spotser, who were followed by Mrs. Tolliver, Mrs. Amos, and
Mrs. Clendenning. Each of them was smiling a big wide smile. Next came Mrs. Ellis
and Reverend Elder from Mount Olive.
They were all smiling big wide smiles. Last
of all came Mr. Jellife and Donna Jean, and
they were smiling too.

When they arrived at their building,
there was Mr. Anderson in front, talking to
some neighbors. He was smiling, too, and
looking very proud because he had already
heard the news of the Three X's triumph.

"Oh, by the way, Mrs. Anderson," Mrs.
Jenkins said as she started in the door. "Jasper can keep that old washtub. I won't be
needing it any more."

"Oh yes, Jasper can keep that scrub
pail, too," Mrs. Spotser said. "I think he put
it to very good use."

"Come to think of it," Mr. Jellife said,
"I just remembered that I have another
broom handle in the basement. Jasper can

have that one. I won't be needing it." And he busied himself with his mop and pail.

The other neighbors went inside.

Mrs. Ellis, Jasper's teacher spoke, "Mrs. Anderson, I am sure that if Jasper takes lessons he won't find it necessary to drum in school. I know if he applies himself, a place can be found for him in the school band. The same is true for Butch and Ike."

"Oh, Brother and Sister Anderson," Reverend Elder said. "Be sure and bring that fine young man of yours to service Sunday. The congregation will be happy to meet a boy who is blessed with such a rare musical gift."

Then Mrs. Ellis and Reverend Elder went their ways.

"See you tomorrow, Jasper," Butch and Ike said, and they give him the secret handshake.

When they were upstairs Mrs. Anderson called Jasper and said, "Jasper dear, run up to the hardware store and get me some more cake tins. You won't need to return the others."

"Thank you, Momma," Jasper said. "And I'll hurry back, too."

Mrs. Anderson sat down in the flowered chair and told Mr. Anderson in detail everything that had happened. "You know, James," she said, "I guess I am to blame for all he's been through. You know how much I like the piano."

"I'm sure, Alice, that the piano lessons haven't done him any harm. In fact, I think they have helped him."

"I'll see Mr. Patton about the drumming lessons too."

"Good," said Mr. Anderson, and he winked up at the Duke Oliver Windy City Band picture. "And, Alice . . . is Father's medal still in the trunk?"

"It was the last time."

"I just wanted to be sure."

Jasper came in with the cake tins. Mrs.

Anderson took them and went back to the kitchen with Donna Jean following. Mr. Anderson sat back in his plum-colored chair and opened the newspaper to the sports page. Jasper sat down on the piano stool and looked up at Grandpa. Grandpa was smiling a big wide smile and so was Duke Oliver and all the other members of the Windy City Band.